Edited by Debbie Lines
Designed by Brigitte Willgoss

ISBN 0 86112 803 6
© Brimax Books Ltd 1989
All rights reserved.
Brimax Paperbacks edition first published 1990.
Third printing 1992.
Brimax Paperbacks is an imprint of Brimax Books Ltd,
Newmarket, England.
Printed in Portugal.

Teddy's
Red Nose

by Diane Jackman

Illustrated by Tina Hancocks

BRIMAX PAPERBACKS

Mrs Harper's toyshop was in the corner of the square.
It was full of toys.
Edward was a teddy bear who had good ideas.
Rory the lion slept all the time.
Clara was a very floppy ragdoll who wished she could dance.

Tom, the soldier boy stood at
the back of the band with his
big bass drum.
"She's here again," he thought,
as he watched a little girl
at the shop window.
"I wonder what she wants,"
thought Edward. "She was here
yesterday."

The shop door opened
and the little girl came in.
"Hello, Mrs Harper," said the little girl.
"How much is that Teddy?"
She pointed to Edward.
"It's my birthday tomorrow and
my Grandma has promised to buy
me a toy."
Mrs Harper took Edward from
his shelf and gave him to
the little girl.

The little girl laughed as she pressed
Edward's back and made him growl.
"He's lovely," she said. "I'll come
back tomorrow with my Grandma."
Mrs Harper put Edward back on
the shelf.
"That was close," thought Edward.
"We can't lose Edward," thought Tom.
"What will we do without Edward?"
thought Clara.

At six o'clock Mrs Harper closed
the shop and went upstairs.
The toys sat and waited.
The cuckoo clock on the shelf
struck seven o'clock, eight o'clock,
nine, ten, eleven.
The clock struck midnight
and began to glow.
The cuckoo came out
and called three times.
''Cuckoo! Cuckoo! Cuckoo!''

The toys came to life,
all talking at once.
''What can we do, Edward?''
''You can't be sold, Edward.''
''I shall miss you,'' said Marietta,
the ballerina in the musical box.
''I don't want to go,'' said Edward.
He sat with his head in his paws.

"You could hide," said Clara.
So Edward hid in the doll's house,
but his arm stuck out.
He hid under a desk,
but his foot stuck out.
There was nowhere for Edward
to hide.

"I'm just too big to hide,"
said Edward. "But it was
a very good idea," he added
when he saw Clara's sad face.
"Now what shall I do?"
He looked at the jack-in-the-box.
"I've got an idea," he said,
clapping his paws together.

"I need a red nose from
the party box," said Edward.
"And some paint and
some funny clothes from
the dressing-up box."
Clara painted Edward's face
black and white.
He looked just like a clown.

Edward put on the funny clothes
and he put on the red nose.
"You look just like the
jack-in-the-box," said Tom,
when Edward was ready.
"I wouldn't buy you," said Clara.
"That's what I wanted to hear,"
said Edward.

The first light of dawn crept
through the window.
The cuckoo came out
and called three times.
The toys stopped moving and talking.
The magic was over for the night.
"I hope this works," thought Edward.
"I hope he isn't sold," thought Tom.
"What will we do if we lose Edward?"
thought Clara as she flopped down.

Later that morning the little girl
came into the shop with her Grandma.
"I've come for the teddy bear,"
she said.
Mrs Harper looked for Edward.
So did the little girl.
So did her Grandma.
The teddy bear was not to be seen.
"There's only this funny looking
clown," said Mrs Harper,
holding Edward.

"I don't want a clown with a black and white face and a red nose," said the little girl. "I'll choose something else."
She looked around the shop.
At last she chose a bright red spinning top with a red handle.
She left the shop very happy.
The toys were happy too.
They still had Edward.

Say these words again

window	desk
girl	hide
birthday	foot
laugh	sad
tomorrow	clown
midnight	white
paws	funny

What can you see?

doll's house

jack-in-the-box

red nose

paint

clothes